Phewtus
the Squirrel

Printed in Hong Kong by South China Printing Company.

First U.S. Edition 1987.
1 2 3 4 5 6 7 8 9 10

Library of Congress Cataloging in Publication Data
Drummond, V. H.
Phewtus the squirrel.
Summary: A knitted squirrel has a chance to become real for a while
and learns he vastly prefers life as a toy.
[1. Squirrels—Fiction. 2. Toys—Fiction] I. Title.
PZ7.D83Ph   1987   [E]   86-18623
ISBN 0-688-07013-2

Phewtus
the Squirrel

V. H. Drummond

Lothrop, Lee & Shepard Books
New York

Phewtus was a knitted squirrel. His body was knitted with orange wool and stuffed with soft wool.

He lived in the Great City with Julian and Julian's father and mother.

He was King of Julian's toy animals and, occasionally, he was allowed to wear his crown, which was rather heavy and weighed his head down a bit.

None of the other toys was envious of Phewtus being King. He had been made King because Julian loved him best of all.

The other toys stood round him and said, "For he's a jolly good fellow," and other patriotic sayings.

Phewtus always did everything with Julian. He slept in his cot and sat in his high chair, and every day he rode in his pram to the Park.

In the Park Julian got out of the pram and ran about or fed the ducks, and talked to the people he knew.

Phewtus had to stay in the pram so that Julian wouldn't drop him in the water or drag him in the mud. He did not like staying in the pram because he felt rather small. Besides, people did not look at him when Julian wasn't there.

One day as he sat there gazing out upon the scene with his vacant bead eyes, a huge puff of wind came and blew him right out of the pram.

He landed under a tree that had snow-drops and crocuses growing around it.

He thought how pleasant it was to loll about amongst the crocuses in the sunshine.

He had not been there long when a grey squirrel came and sat down beside him to eat a piece of bread.

Phewtus was very frightened at first, but when he had overcome his astonishment, he said: "Who are you?"

"I'm Furtail, the grey squirrel," was the reply.

"I am a squirrel too," said Phewtus.

Hearing this, Furtail sprang up and gave a shout of laughter.

"What! You a squirrel?" he cried, pointing his paw at him.

Poor Phewtus was very much offended at this and started to cry.

Seeing Phewtus's tears, Furtail was sorry and said, "Never mind, I expect it is quite nice to be a stuffed woollen squirrel; but it is great fun to be a real squirrel and caper all over the Park and jump from tree to tree."

"I should like to do that," said Phewtus gravely.

"Very well," said Furtail, "I will turn you into a real squirrel – a red one."

Phewtus was very much excited by these words, but he said: "I could never leave Julian, he would be so unhappy without me."

"Nonsense," said Furtail. "I will meet you tomorrow." He skipped away and disappeared into the tree tops.

Just at that moment Phewtus heard a
great commotion going on round Julian's
pram. People were calling, "Phewtus!
Phewtus!" and looking for him everywhere.

"I'm lost," said Phewtus, feeling startled. But while he was wondering how he could get back, all the people looked up and saw him sitting under the tree.

"There he is," they shouted, and ran to him.

They brought him back to Julian, who was crying by the pram. He was very pleased to see Phewtus again and kissed him.

At home there was a surprise waiting for Julian. A large parcel. In it was a present from Father, a huge dressed rabbit called Ralph.

Ralph was the most conceited toy that had ever been made. All the other toys hated him on sight.

He immediately decided to make himself King and dethrone Phewtus. He was very proud of being dressed in his red velvet dressing gown, and kept on showing off to Julian.

He even managed to sit in Julian's high chair. But he was so large that he had to be removed, and all the other toys said: "Good."

That night he got into Julian's bed and lay down. Poor Phewtus was left lying on the floor.

The next day he insisted on going to the Park. Julian was very amused with Ralph, and kept on making Phewtus kiss him.

(Look at the insufferable smile on Ralph's face.)

When they got to the Park, Ralph pushed Phewtus out of the pram.

No one noticed this except Furtail, who was standing nearby.

"Now will you let me turn you into a real squirrel?" he said.

Phewtus was so angry at the way he'd been treated that he agreed.

"I have brought my magic stick with me," said Furtail. Phewtus looked at the magic stick. It was a little sycamore twig, with a sycamore nut hanging on the end of it.

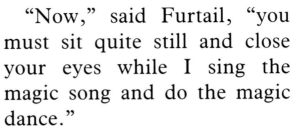

"Now," said Furtail, "you must sit quite still and close your eyes while I sing the magic song and do the magic dance."

Phewtus sat quite still with his back against a tree.

Then Furtail, waving his magic stick, started to dance: one hop to the right, two to the left, pivot. He did this five times, singing as he did so:

> "Phewtus, Phewtus,
>   squirrel be.
> Hop and skip from
>   tree to tree."

When the performance was finished he said, "Open your eyes, Phewtus."

Phewtus opened his eyes. He looked down and saw that his orange body had gone, and that he was covered with brownish red fur. He felt his face and found that he had whiskers sticking out from it, and that his ears were soft and furry.

Suddenly, he gave a great spring and landed half-way up the tree. In two seconds he was at the topmost branch gazing down on the people below.

Then he sprang through the air and landed on the next tree.

From there he went on, springing from tree to tree, till he had been all round the Park three times, without ever touching the ground.

"I am so happy," he said to himself. "I am a real animal, made of fur."

All at once a great wind blew in the trees. The sun disappeared and gusts of rain fell out of the clouds. Phewtus felt the branch he was sitting on sway and creak, and a burst of thunder clapped out of the sky.

He ran down the tree. "I'm frightened," he said. He folded his arms about himself and felt his fur wet and cold on his body. He had a queer pain inside him which he realized must be hunger. He had never known cold and hunger when he was a stuffed squirrel.

He thought of Julian, who would now be having tea in his cosy house.

"I must find Furtail," he said. So he ran off through the rain calling: "Furtail, Furtail."

But the wind blew so that Phewtus could not hear his own voice. The ground was wet and he slipped in the puddles.

Suddenly night fell, and black darkness descended. Night animals came out and started screaming and shouting in the wind.

By this time Phewtus was so frightened that he lay down by a tree and covered his eyes.

As he lay shivering with fear and cold, he heard the tramp of human feet and, looking up, he saw Morton, the Park Keeper, trudging through the rain.

Somehow he managed to creep up and fall exhausted at Morton's feet.

Morton picked Phewtus up and carried him back to his lodge, where his wife made him a little warm nest in her knitting basket to sleep in, and gave him some milk.

While Phewtus was asleep Furtail came with his little sycamore twig and changed him back into a toy squirrel.

So when the Park Keeper and his wife came back to the basket in the morning, they were surprised to see a stuffed woollen squirrel before their eyes.

"Someone has played a trick on us," they exclaimed. "They have stolen our squirrel and put this thing here in its place."

Phewtus was not very pleased at being called a thing, but he was too happy to be a toy again to care.

"I shall not rest," said Morton, "till I find our little red squirrel and have the wicked one who stole him punished."

So he went to the Park with Phewtus under his arm and said to everyone he saw: "Did you steal my red squirrel last night and put this thing in his place?"

Everyone was very indignant and said: "No."

But when they saw how distressed he was about losing his little red squirrel, they forgave him.

Morton searched about amongst the trees
and bushes and flowers, but could not find
his squirrel anywhere.

When he got home for lunch, his wife said: "Well?" But she could see by his forlorn attitude that he had had no luck.

"You must search again this afternoon," she said, and gave him a huge helping of roly-poly pudding; but he was so unhappy he couldn't eat it.

Meanwhile, in Julian's house, there was a fine pandemonium going on. All the toys were weeping noisily and crying, "Where is Phewtus? Where is he?"

Julian was crying and crying and he could not eat his lunch. They had all cried and wailed so much the night before that no one could sleep.

When Father heard that Phewtus was missing, he said, "I will buy a real squirrel for Julian, and then he will stop crying."

So the next morning he went to a shop where they sold mice and other little animals, and bought a real live red squirrel in a little house.

Now most people would have been very pleased to have a real squirrel in a house, but not Julian. He was so unhappy about losing Phewtus that he took no notice of it, but just went on crying.

They called the new squirrel "Sprite" because of his dainty, darting manners.

All this time Ralph sat with Phewtus's crown on his head. Now that he was King, he was rather bored with the position, because no one took any notice of him, and when Mother suggested that Julian should take him to the Park with them that afternoon, Julian refused because he said he was sick of him. So Mother put Sprite and his house in the pram instead.

As soon as Julian was in the Park he jumped out of his pram and started looking for Phewtus. He searched all over the paths and lawns.

He asked people to rise from their chairs in case they were sitting on him.

He even peered under the leaves of the water lilies that grew in the pond.

He went so far as to rummage about in the flower-beds, and the gardeners, who should have been cross, saw how sad he was and forgave him.

Meanwhile, Sprite was beginning to get tired of his house and, by cleverly putting his paw through the window, he managed to open the door and hop out. He felt rather frightened, alone in a great park, and timidly sprang to the top of a weeping willow tree.

The first person to see him was Morton, who, thinking he was his lost squirrel, climbed up after him. A great crowd gathered and said, "Look at the Park Keeper up the tree."

Julian who was still looking for Phewtus, became involved in the crowd, and as he tried to crawl out, Phewtus fell on his head.

"Phewtus, Phewtus, where did you come from?" he cried.

He thought that Phewtus had dropped out of the clouds, but Phewtus had really fallen out of Morton's pocket as he climbed down the weeping willow tree with Sprite in his hand.

As the crowd dispersed, Morton broke through, singing: "I've found my sweet pet."

Julian watched him and thought: He is as happy to find his squirrel as I am to find Phewtus.

Then Julian ran back to his pram with
Phewtus. When he got there he found that
Sprite had vanished. Suddenly he realized
that the Park Keeper had mistaken Sprite
for another squirrel, but, being a very kind
little boy, he did not say anything about it.

Instead, he ran to the lodge and gave
Sprite's house to the Park Keeper and his
wife. "Thank you," they said. "Now our
squirrel will not get lost again."

When Julian got home he told Mother and Father and the toys all that had happened. Everyone was so pleased to have Phewtus home again that they did not mind about Sprite leaving them.

Ralph, who was sick of being King with no one taking any notice of him, gave the crown back to Phewtus, and said, "I am sorry for my insufferable behaviour towards you."

"You are forgiven," Phewtus said kindly and kissed him.

Then Phewtus sat in the place of honour, with his crown upon his head, while Julian and his Mother and Father and all the toys danced round him to express their joy. Phewtus felt very happy to be home and thought how nice it was to be a stuffed knitted woollen squirrel again after his great adventure.